Deep Work
For 坤(Gon: Ground)*

---

*坤 is the name of one of the four divination signs represented on the
Korean flag, ☷ symbolizing Earth

Deep Work

A collection of new poems by An Hyeon-Mi
Translated by Brother Anthony of Taizé

POET

아시아

Contents

DEEP WORK

Deep Work

From that day on, someone is enduring the ocean for a whole lifetime.

It is deep work.

A night drinking today's last cup of coffee.

Somehow, in this lifetime, I will have to be irresponsible.

Like a heart left neglected for a long time that one day disappeared, like hatred dragged about for a long time that one day became useless,

somehow this life will have to die first,

then any time left will have to live life.

Somehow this life will have to live as a person eating alone, crying alone, then die.
that is deep work.

Sewol Ferry Modbot

I write that in order to end I must begin. I write that I begin although I know that it will end. So I write that the Sewol ferry should only have sunk into the sea at Maeng-gol where nothing but special measures and high-class nonsense that will have to be refashioned float like buoys. I write that there are mothers only longing to know the truth who endured sorrowfully for over a hundred days from the entrance of tears to the entrance of despair. Now I write urging an end to efforts at such measures, such tears. I write demanding an end to the worst. I write demanding an end to false hope, no matter what or who. I write that progressive and conservative were both far away. I write that I want to live side by side with the beloved names. I write that I want to die. I write that the words 'I miss you' have turned into so many nails hammered into me. I write that having said I would sell anything to raise money I really have sold everything. I write that I have even sold hell. I write that no matter what or who should be hammered into the words '**I miss my kids.**' I write that I die and die yet cannot die. I write that I must begin again until I die and die and die again.

#YoSoy132

That mouth must **shut up** #YoSoy132 I am face number 132. The mouth which said that all had been saved when none could be saved must **shut up**. Even the pitiful mouth pouring out bleeding words, words that stab like the dagger of a mother saying she longs to see her kids again, must **shut up**. The mouth that told our kids to stay put, the mouth that cannot restore to them the spring it robbed them of must **shut up**. #WeareSewolhonumber305, you want us to stop? For what? To sink again? To stay incompetent? That mouth must **shut up**. That blind mouth must **shut up**. Before I stick a dagger in that shamelessness that mouth must **shut up**. The mouths of those bastards who are not my kids who can never come back to life must **shut up**.

Tree on a School Trip*

A tree is writing. It writes that we are all impli-
cated, that we will never be able to set off, not in
winter, not in spring, not in summer, not in autumn,
not on Wednesday, not on Wednesday, not on
Wednesday. It writes that ultimately there is nothing capable of setting off. That tears have simply
dried up.

A tree is crying. A tree is crying for the sorrow of
those who climbed up chimneys, up pylons, above
dictatorship, of the survivors. Saying that we are all
causes and fools.

* Inspired by a poem by Lee Young-kwang

A tree is advancing. Through darkness, straddling rocks, beyond classes, a tree is advancing. In search of tears, toward the heart of tears, for solidarity with the tears, a tree is advancing. Toward April's April sea.

A tree is flying. The world is always critically ill but I'm leaving on our school trip. I will remember. I will keep record. I want to live. I love you, Mom. Not loved because special but grown special because of loving, recalling and recording that love, the tree flies on. The tree will go soaring aloft.

A Spell

Lucky it rained. Lucky there's music.

Lucky there's been two unlucky things and one lucky.

Lucky spring has come. Lucky there's the plaza.

Lucky there are several questions and one written decision.

National Pigeon Unity, Zebra Language Research Group, Confederation of Cat Unions, American Raccoon Federation Korean Branch, Tiger's Meow Association, National Stay-at-home Type Union, People Alone, Aquarium Sans Frontières, Muhan Co. Workers' Union, Rhino Beetle Re-

search Association . . . . . .

Feet were drunk enough to become hands.

Walls were drunk enough to become doors.

Is this all because of me?

An impenitent

drunkard sitting after writing this poem, drunk.

It was no dream

That winter I dreamed that someone paid for a question

mark for me, someone paid for an exclamation mark for

me. Not a dog-dream, not a pig-dream, a punctuation-mark-dream, an impeachment, is all this a dream?

Moon. But are we going toward revolution like going to the square?

Unexpectedly White

A green local bus went by, and there was a woman wearing a floral dress, and the future had arrived, but the idea was not as advanced as we thought, though being warm-hearted and being heartless are both the work of human beings, once Saturday came round we went out to the square. In the meantime, conglomerates and high civil servants went to jail. If I had to lose love and people, I reckoned I would be able to stop myself. Meanwhile, we poor folk expanded into we beautiful folk and finally that got quoted and a thrilling fireworks display colored the dark night sky above the square. Being warm-hearted and being heartless are both the work of human beings, and though life was not as advanced as we thought, still an unexpectedly white, radical magnolia was coming.

Marae Tunnel

I've seen the shadow of a coachman rubbing the shadow of a coach with the shadow of a brush. (Dostoyevsky, "*The Karamazov Brothers*")

What tunnel are we going through? I said it was a tunnel that people built in the Japanese colonial time. One day you asked me what period I would like to visit if I could ride a time machine. There was nowhere I wanted to go but I did not want to disappoint you when you were so full of expectation so I said that I wanted to go back to the time when Dostoyevsky was writing "*The Karamazov Brothers*." But

I said I didn't know what century that was. I might add that I seemed to be a shadow someone keeps dragging around, or something like that, a stain or trace. What would it feel like to become someone in the Japanese colonial time? I asked, if you could use a time machine one day, what period would you like to visit? You replied, a period when there are people building a tunnel of despair using hammers and chisels. I said we should visit the shadows of Marae building the shadows of a tunnel with the shadows of words.

Hi, Yellow.

You said, there has to be someone who endures, so you should endure. Please endure, you said. Please survive, you said. Please survive and keep record for a long, long time, you said. I wondered if I would be capable, but you roared that that is a problem of poetic and anti-poetic solitude, not a worldly problem of regular and irregular, conservative and progressive, wealth and power. Oddly enough, I began to feel that I could endure a little longer.

Time breeding time is keeping record of everything.

The Competence of Incompetence

The woman took Monday out of her bag. The woman who rode the subway like a possessed shaman dancing frantically on cutter blades, her face crumpling, tramping through ten years, a business purpose contract worker for three years, an unlimited contract worker for five years, a regular worker for two years, the woman who every year when the wild ginger flowers bloomed wrote a letter of resignation then tore it up, repeating then reversing it, the woman who frantically set off for work after storing her heart frozen in seven pieces in the freezer, the woman who kept losing her way between past life and approaching life, the woman who went about with solitude in one eye, poetry in the other, the woman now erased from the world of regular employment, the woman fond of Jorge Luis Borges, Park Sang-ryung, Huh Su-Kyung, the woman who has never claimed as much shadow of a shadow as anyone drags around, the woman who came to realize that in trust is treason and that even without hope wild ginger flowers bloom, the woman who decided to thaw out her heart frozen in seven pieces, even if it meant she became poorer and more incompetent,

A Scapegoat

A long-awaited Sunday

Some times are like clouds

This sorrow provoked allergies

"Chew it well. Whatever it is."

I close the window and open my eyes

How does becoming death feel?

A long-awaited Sunday

Some sheep are like clouds

Like the fingerprints that everyone has

Like the questions everyone asks

I wipe away my tears and open my eyes

How does becoming death feel?

"Chew it well. Whatever it is"

A Solitary Life

Sunday is deep like a cave. I like the sound of the pressure being released from a pressure cooker as much as Beethoven's "Destiny" Fifth Symphony. It sounds like music being sung by a scattered family. Sunday is like music. A cross is like wings. An angel's wings. Someone dumped an unbroken mirror beneath a cross, a version of the Passion. I went into the mirror as if going to church and repented for a while before going home. I was engulfed in doubts. Sunday was good like someone set free, despite the pain. I hadn't been able to live very well, but I would not live very badly. Although I only had a thousand-won note in my wallet, and had experienced erasure at the hands of one I loved deeply, a Sunday when I wanted to repent over and over again, a Sunday warm like a pressure cooker with the pressure released, a Sunday of prayer and thanksgiving for this life in which I can exert no pressure anywhere in the world, Sunday is Sunday, even read backwards, therefore a Sunday wishing to keep reading backwards, a Sunday neither free nor paying, carrying lives in which we were able to love like collection a baskets, we

Metamorphosis
-Subaltern

The time spent weeping loudly, calling his father who had not returned from the coalface, the time taken for a nickel-silver lunchbox to grow warm on top of a stove, the time taken to go roaming the pharmacy alley collecting sleeping pills

We are from another time

A dimension as small as a mosquito buzz, a dimension where although we decided that I should live and you should live, we never decided that you should be killed and I should live, a dimension where poverty, winter and discrimination overflowed equally.

We are from another dimension

Neither alive nor dead, like chopped octopus as a bar snack, dogs, pigs, women, refugees . . . . Worse than a brute to anyone, my friendly social ranks like bar snacks, born but obliged to live as if dead

We are from different classes

The bear will take us.
The bear will take us.*

* The last lines are adapted from "The wind will take us" by Forugh Farrokhzad.

Taebaek

After much effort, the bear finally became special,

like a woman who became special in love, not who

loved because she was special.

The darkness of a blind end at a coalface

Lovers who are beautiful but unfaithful

Love's North

Worse than a brute to anyone

Mother is changing coal briquettes

Blood circulates

Obliged to go a long way

Obliged to go a long way

From bear to girl

Synopsis for a Threepenny Opera

Beside that restaurant's pepper shaker there is a colored pencil. When I think of the lack of expression on the face of the woman pulling at the thread of a maroon pencil, I feel immensely sad. She is doing it as a woman, as a young woman, but is doing it as a young woman who never once appears. She is making a puzzle with a scrap of a dream. It's the problem of a fragment of fate that will always be lost. It is not a problem of whether to live or die but of whether to die or die like a dog. An angel's wings are like the transformation of a cross. Fated to fail day after day in order to draw closer to perfection. What are we? When are we? The fate of a woman squandering her life getting drunk on cheap liquor, emerges three times and withdraws three times, like the cuckoo of a cuckoo clock announcing three in the afternoon. Beside that restaurant's pepper shaker there is a colored pencil. She is doing it as a woman who is sitting impotently pulling at the thread of a maroon pencil. But she does it as an old woman who never once withdraws.

Maybe we're all involved in a maroon nightmare.

A Drunkard

One winter's night I sit like a birch tree and drink with a man who just came back from Sakhalin. For some time now, he has been talking about a certain time. Talk about a strange time that never grows any larger or smaller, does not flow and does not stop, talk about how that kind of thing is not love, that there is absolutely no such thing as a future, talk as dirty and gray as a cotton swab thrown away in a vacant lot, talk that therefore keeps growing more opaque, talk like a drunkard who routinely keeps losing the spell releasing him from a curse, or rather talk of finally becoming a drunkard saying he is enduring what nobody can endure above an ellipse or in another, fearing he might turn into a trickster only capable of committing a crime such as speeding or illegal parking with a nuance of suicide, he had decided to become a drunkard, and someone dumped the broken man beneath a cross like an angel's wings, or a version of the Passion.

Hi, Bear

Have you ever seen a bear cutting and pasting time? Obviously it never once thought of accepting its lifelong hibernation as fate, it was no orphan but was like an orphan, and now there was a bear that firmly believed it could become the god of this world, being the only one who knew that that spring sunlight shining on its scissors as it cut up forty-nine winters after breaking the curse given as fate, like it or not, was the curse of curses. *Obviously you're crazy! You keep saying that the future and women are always the problem. I'm neither the future nor a transman. Wait! Can I borrow you tonight? You say nobody can borrow death but isn't there some other way? I want you to focus on your work, we got along so well drinking together in the spring, yeuk yeuk yeuk.* Have you ever seen a bear cutting and pasting a curse? What is obvious is night, night is coming.

A Round Night

I like speeding along the highway at dawn

the street lights shining though nobody's looking

dark and quiet, the street-side trees, and

hours that will never come again

no need to arrive anywhere

heading for a love that exists nowhere

believing that somewhere in the speeding darkness

there is the sea

speeding along the highway at dawn

a night

when the unexpected greeting of the April sea

mingles their bodies

when both life and death

are round

A Full-Length Mirror

Who is that man with a camera who shows up every night in my dreams?

Who is that woman who every night hands Monday to that man?

That was an allegory that failed to become an allegory.

There's a man who goes to the North Pole on an icebreaker,

as well as a woman, sentimental in autumn, who

stays at work until nine o'clock.

Surely, you need to accept it, to be a sea?

We need to talk sense.

One autumn.

Two autumns.

Three autumns.

I confess. I am dead.

I'm dead yet keep coming to work.

I confess. I am someone who goes to work.

I am someone who goes to work yet keeps dying.

We need to talk sense.

That woman draws Monday out of a full-length mirror.

That was an allegory that failed to become an allegory.

Gi-Hyang's Noodles

A man back from the mainland is cooking noodles.

Two bowls of noodles.

Two bowls of noodles.

As for love, he finally has to pass through love,

unable to turn his back on one woman for a long
time,

after turning his back, with plenty of space still left,

Gi-hyang, back from the mainland, is cooking noodles.

Slurp slurp

Slurp slurp

As for love, finally love has to be swallowed scald-
ing hot,
unable to turn my back on one man for a long
time,
I had to let them be as they are inevitably,
what regret, what anxiety, and what embarrass-
ment.

Snow is falling tonight.
Inevitably there is a back cooking noodles.
Inevitably there is a sorrowful night

There Being Clouds

The name of a northern fish is

Ground.

After the fish comes a bird.

The name of the bird is Roc.

The season glimpsed

wearing Hyojin's smart 3D glasses is multinational

Like a pig with twenty-eight nipples

endlessly eating, feeding, being eaten

Mon, Tue, Wed, Thu, Fri, Fri, Fri,

undoubtedly one single death

the name of the northern cloud is

Extinction.

POET'S NOTES

I can do it, too.

Everything began because of those words.

So it gave me a reason not to surrender in the face of any sadness or any despair. Because of those ordinary, impossible to forget, unforgettable words that anyone can say I was able to become a poet like a Walt Whitman, congratulating myself and cel- ebrating myself.

"Shut up!"

After that day, someone has been enduring that sea for the rest of their life. Today we are barely alive. Maybe a curse is the easiest form of forgiveness. That's right. I'm going to have to live and die as a poet who grieves for the sea and celebrates the sea.

You say you could love but could not exceed love. As you gaze at the deep dark sea and sob that you miss your kids so much, you wanted to die instead of them if you could, you say. That the cross is like a suffering version of angels' wings. It's a scary, lonesome, utterly lonely spring

Indeed so. If we have to lose love, people, it is a night for thinking that we should stop people.

"I will keep record."

Some kinds of sorrow depart at dawn and some kinds of pain can never return. Since that day we have been nailed to that sea. You say, I so want to see my kids who are like angels nailed to the sea. I will not forget. Though they are forgotten I will not forget. I will remember and keep record. Indeed so. We can do it. I'm going to have to die after dying as a poet who grieves for the sea and celebrates the sea.

POET'S ESSAY

The Bow and the Lyre

1. Acrostic Poem

An. I'm going to bring out the landscape inside me. Pixel flown off at the moment of making. Incomplete video. **Hyeon**. I must hold onto the Sage's Stone. A ritual that grew desiccated everywhere I went. Incomplete space. **Mi**. I resembled Mimosa's nerves. Neurons have erections every time they doubt. Incomplete time. Booting failure. Search for hidden meanings or hidden names.

2. Hyeon(String)

Instruments that resound even without strings. For example, round pebbles in rivers, a cottonwood tree before a summer breeze, a woman standing beside love, eating boiled angelica shoots at the dinner table, a suitcase that comes back after wandering in an unknown place, a waxing moon floating over a thousand rivers, the tail of a fish swimming toward its origin, spring just arriving after cutting across winter, a free pass drawn with crayons, a water jar bright with jealousy, a bent old woman running nimbly away after snapping off the eastern branch of the crape myrtle tree in Gaesim-sa temple, clouds that ask questions, a silver bicycle crossing a wooden bridge, an unbridled horse galloping over the inland of language. . .

Those who, even without strings, bring sounds to participate in beauty. My body always wanted to steal that beauty. No. My body always wanted to participate in that beauty. The desire for such participation emerging from my body buried in solid everyday life, taking my soul, suddenly makes me go galloping like an unbridled horse into a river, beside a summer breeze, beside love, onto a dinner table, to an unknown place, to a thousand rivers, to the origin, to spring. On such days I am a pebble and a cottonwood tree and a woman and a dinner table as well as a suitcase, a waxing moon, a fish, spring, night, a cloud that asks questions, a water jar, and the east side of the crape myrtle in Gaesim-sa temple.

3. My Lyres

Bow and lyre share the same string. Despite sharing the same string, the bow becomes a weapon and the lyre becomes music. I am bait caught on such fascination. A target willingly become a target for bows and lyres flying together with unheard-of time. Misfortune and happiness, love and hatred, night and day, summer and winter, life and death, laughter and tears, hell and heaven, gravity and weightlessness, breathing in and breathing out, inside and out, spring and autumn, music and art, mountains and sea, full moon and old moon, girl and old woman, meaning and meaninglessness, train and plane, silence and solitude, Bashō and frog. . . Like the siamese twins born in 18th-century Thailand.

Truth or lie, that divide 'I' in half, like bow and lyre sharing the same string. I earn money by day, write poems at night. No. I am a butterfly by day and Chuang-tzu being dreamed of by a butterfly by night. No. By day, I am Chuang-tzu and by night a butterfly being dreamed of by Chuang-tzu. Lee Sungbok, Borges, Huh Soo-kyung, Quignard, Baek Seok, Sep lveda, Octavio Paz, the Youlhwadang Art Library, the Sigongsa Discovery Series, "*Zorba the Greek,*" "*Che Guevara, A Critical Biography,*" the picture book "*The Giving Tree,*". . . My beautiful lyres. A lovers' dream. A dream about young poets who live and breathe at the same period is a daydream left for unknown you.

4. Mi(beauty) came to Me

Summer that year, which was given a long name, "the day Ann came and rain came, too." Summer, beautiful as a vase and sweet as Fanta. Life is full of esoteric wishes to explore, all seals seal themselves, red grew more deeply red, blue more deeply blue, thick masks melted like vanilla ice cream. The whole world was participating in that summer. I wanted to explain it, but it was a summer that I could not explain. Was it because of you? Was it because of poetry? Ecstatic, insecure, seeming to faint, seeming to fly, crying, smiling, after being clear becoming dreary. Those things rushing in indiscriminately. A beauty that I want to explain but cannot explain. But once Ann had gone and the rain had stopped, a summer that went back to being foam like a beautiful girl born in foam. Nevertheless, the thing I wanted to explain but couldn't explain still remained within me. 美 and 未來, beauty and the future. It was preposterous but the thought struck me that that was poetry. Remembering that beauty that could not be explained despite not being able to be explained. Summer was sealed, but sealed summer turned into poetry.

5. Flower Understanding Words*

A flower understanding words, A poppy. A horse

* In Korean 'mal' means both 'word' and horse' and often there is no way of telling which is the writer's meaning when the word occurs.

understanding words, Half-human, half-horse. Strange and beautiful metaphor.

I own two opaque fish tanks. Body and soul. Those two opaque fish tanks dream of flowers that understand words and horses that understand words becoming infinitely transparent. Desk is desk, summer is is is is is summer. Unbridled horses go galloping across the inland of language. Horses spurring on. Horse-words that make the impossible impossible. I wanted to steal that. No. I wanted to mount a strange and beautiful horse-word, shoot a bow, turn on a lyre and pass over inconvenience. Lonely like an adverb. I wanted to love my half-human and half-inhuman destiny. The bow of that love is poetry, the lyre of that love is poetry. But a flower that may only bloom once after despairing a hundred times. Tragic fate's half-human half-horse. A model disqualified in the 21st century's neoliberal era. Nevertheless, that can't make me sad. I earn money by day and write poetry by night. Write whenever room appears. Make room and write. There is no secret method other than writing. Just, barely, I write.

I'm going to pull out the scenery inside, the pixels that blew away the moment I said that. Incomplete video. I'll hold on with the Sage's Stone. A ritual that dried up everywhere I went. Incomplete space. Neurons that resemble Mimosa's nerves but grow erect whenever they suspect. Incomplete time. Reboot. Inner, brown rice or bow and lyre.

COMMENTARY

Another Shadow about Contingency, Irony, and Solidarity

Jang Ye-won (Literary critic)

1. Making words for those who endure the sea with their remaining lives

In the first few poems of her collection "Deep Work", An Hyeon-mi deals with the sorrow of the Sewol ferry disaster. In particular, through the poems "Deep Work" and "Sewol Ferry ModBot", she professes to be an ironist. I think ironists feel drawn together, not through a common language, but rather through sensitivity to pain, especially to a special kind of pain that animals cannot share with humans, that is, to humiliation. According to Rorty, humanity's solidarity is not a matter of sharing a common truth or a common goal, but a matter of sharing a common private hope, a hope that their world—the little things around which they have woven their final vocabulary—will not be destroyed.

What has been presented as government measures for the Sewol ferry disaster—in other words, "special measures and special thoughtless words" written in a common language and with a facade of common sense—are words that add to the humiliation of the victims of the Sewol ferry and their families. They are just "another measure and another tear" disguised with useless words. These words humiliate those in grief and pain from the loss of their children by making their indescribable despair insignificant, trite, and lethargic, far from sincerely consoling the students who drowned before they even had a chance to be defiled by life. That humiliation is a long-lasting pain for the bereaved families, more acute than the sorrow of losing a child.

Pain mixed with sorrow and humiliation is difficult to verbalize. That is because pain is originally non-verbal. Therefore, the victims—that is, those who suffer—have little to do with language. The usual and sensible language that the victims once used no longer works for them and has no meaning. They are experiencing so much suffering and humiliation that they cannot combine their unfamiliar suffering with existing language. So it is up to others who care for them to express their situation in language. And An Hyeon-mi is trying to do her part as a poet.

I write that in order to end I must begin. I write that I begin although I know that it will end. So I write that the Sewol ferry should only have sunk into the sea at Maeng-gol where nothing but special measures and high-class nonsense that will have to be refashioned float like buoys. I write that there are mothers only longing to know the truth who endured sorrowfully for over a hundred days from the entrance of tears to the entrance of despair. Now I write urging an end to efforts at such measures, such tears. I write demanding an end to the worst. I write demanding an end to false hope, no matter what or who. I write that progressive and conservative were both far away. I write that I want to live side by side with the beloved names. I write that I want to die. I write that the words 'I miss you' have turned into so many nails hammered into me. I write that having said I would sell anything to raise money I really have sold everything. I write that I have even sold hell. I write that no matter what or who should be hammered into the words 'I miss my kids.' I write that I die and die yet cannot die. I write that I must begin again until I die and die and die again.

"Sewol Ferry Modbot" full text

Irony is the opposite of common sense. In a situation where common sense humiliates those in pain, one must respond with irony and "speak a positionless sentence" that can really comfort the victims. For this reason, with the sentences "I write that in order to end I must begin. I write that I begin although I know that it will end" and "somehow this life will have to die first, then any time left will have to live life."(Deep Work), Ahn creates irony and expresses respect and consolation to the victims of the disaster. And by expanding common sensitivity for pain and humiliation with the sentence "the words 'I miss you' have turned into so many nails"(Deep Work) and the phrase "solidarity with the tears"(Tree on a School Trip), she creates a true social bond and solidarity that amends "special measures and special thoughtless words." She wants to uphold her poetic principle as an ironist that solidarity must be a matter of finding something that is already there, but be composed of tiny fragments of the basic language we all can understand when we hear it. (Richard Rorty)

This poetic principle that she upholds as an ironist is revealed and expanded not only through the Sewol victims, but also through metaphors: "Neither alive nor dead, like chopped octopus as a bar snack, dogs, pigs, women, refugees . . . . Worse than a brute to anyone, my friendly social ranks like bar snacks, born but obliged to live as if dead."("Metamorphosis").

2. Are we going toward revolution like going to the square?

The French Revolution is a case in which words in the spectrum of social relations and social institutions changed in just a few days. This revolution showed people that utopian politics is not merely an ideal but can be realized as a reality. Utopian politics dreams of creating new forms of society, leaving behind questions about human nature that resembles God's will.

In the Korea of the 2000s, it is difficult to realize a huge "revolution" in which the entire vocabulary of social relations and systems are reversed in a short period of time. An Hyeon-mi also knows this. So she doesn't ask, "Can we realize a revolution?" but asks, "are we going toward revolution?"("A Spell") And this question also contains a change resulting from the reason that the process and procedures to get to a revolution may be more important than getting to a revolution itself. In an era where a revolution is impossible, the road to a revolution is in the form of "Life Culture Advancement" where we can inde-pendently decide and share what we want and what we can quit, rather than in the form of wild changes associated with huge systems. Going to a revolution, or going to a square, is not a special or macroscopic thing, but rather an ordinary routine where one can see a "green local bus" or "a woman wearing a floral dress." This is not a struggle for struggle's sake, or a revolution for revolution as ideology or concept, but a present improvement in the quality of autonomy in life, and we can approach a revolution with poetic words like "Rose Community" and "unexpectedly white, radical magnolia." These two terms are new expressions that combine politics and art and become a world view in which politics can also be realized through art. This is the realization of Richard Rorty's proposition, "If we take care of freedom, the truth will help itself" and this is also a creative act that converts old and clichéd democratic concepts into new and fresh terms of democracy.

A green local bus went by, and there was a woman wearing a floral dress, and the future had arrived, but the idea was not as advanced as we thought, though being warm-hearted and being heartless are both the work of human beings, once Saturday came round we went out to the square. In the meantime, conglomerates and high civil servants went to jail. If I had to lose love and people, I reckoned I would be able to stop myself. Meanwhile, we poor folk expanded into we beautiful folk and finally that got quoted and a thrilling fireworks display colored the dark night sky above the square. Being warm-hearted and being heartless are both the work of human beings, and though life was not as advanced as we thought, still an unexpectedly white, radical magnolia was coming.

"Unexpectedly White" full text

The speaker in the poem "Unexpectedly White" is aware that "the future had arrived, but the idea was not as advanced as we thought." The speaker goes to "the square" every Saturday as if to enjoy a festival in order not to lose "love and people" in everyday life, rather than chasing after the vanity of the thoughts and the future Utopian politics dreams of. When we independently do what we can and should do now and here in everyday space and share it through the network, the "poor folk" expands into the "beautiful folk." It is the concrete process and substance of the road leading to a revolution and we can always experience it in the present. It is also a way of leaving the finite nature of a system that always delays and sacrifices what we want and can do now for the future that may be a fiction.

3. "#Yosoy132"—endlessly repetitive re-description

Everyone has their own vocabulary to explain their beliefs, their deeds, and ultimately their lives. Those words span the various rites of passage in life, such as love for family, longing for a lover, cursing the hated, skepticism about one's identity, and future wishes. They are words that describe the trajectory of our lives, which we looked forward to with hopes, expectations and sometimes anxiety, and looked back on with longing and regret. Our lives are true or false as far as we describe them in our own vocabulary and share them. Life or the world itself is neither moral nor immoral. To find a reasonable way to respond to the world, one must use a living vocabulary of one's own "will or feeling" to give a verbal narrative of the world and share it with others. When we do this, we can make the world moral or immoral and this is why we are allowed to "agree or disagree but should not be silent"("Deep Matter"). The point, however, is that there are no objective and subjective norms here, as is the case with "going to a revolution." It is entirely autonomous and therefore accidental.

The act of describing each other from different

positions makes clear that none of us is in a privileged position against anyone. Describing someone and citing someone through multiple, simultaneous networks, makes the person or others give up the idea that there is a privileged perspective by which to describe themselves or others, contributing to "going to a revolution." This way and attitude acts as a mechanism that, without requiring reliance on authority or power, offers the position of speaker or narrator to "The woman who rode the subway like a possessed shaman dancing frantically on cutter blades, her face crumpling, tramping through ten years, a business purpose contract worker for three years, an unlimited contract worker for five years, a regular worker for two years," "the woman who has never claimed as much shadow of a shadow,"("The Competence of Incompetence"), "a life in which I can exert no pressure anywhere in the world"("A Solitary Life"), and "not a problem of whether to live or die but of whether to die or die like a dog"("Synopsis for a Threepenny Opera"). As everyone becomes information producers, remixers and retweeters, they enjoy the contingency of phenomena, overcome authority without showing off authority, and exceed power without relying on the ambitions of those in power.

In the 2000s, Korean society is clearly a problem-free, problematic world filled with "a strange time that never grows any larger or smaller, does not flow and does not stop, talk about how that kind of thing is not love, that there is absolutely no such thing as a future"("A Drunkard"). In a world full of talk of "no such thing as a future," An Hyeon-mi does not try to fill the gap between phenomena and reality, time and eternity, language and the non-verbal. "I'm dead yet keep coming to work"("A Full-Length Mirror") and "now erased from the world of regular employment"("Incompetence of Incompetence") maintain a poetic attitude that does not chase after a macroscopic prospect or the future that may be an illusion. Yet the women are not lethargic but full of energy. Even if they become "poorer and more incompetent," they decide to thaw their frozen hearts, seven hearts for seven days a week. There's no hidden truth to be discovered in the world; maybe sorrow, longing, and hatred all are "a work of hormones"; and they've been feeling cold at heart because of "hunger for warm noodles"("Menopause"). They find these "at a noodle place." And that bowl of "warm noodles" can become the strength and truth to endure the era where, while a revolution is impossible, going to a revolution is possible.

So An Hyeon-mi goes to the past instead of the future. Perhaps, it is because she realized that describing the past can be a creative act that creates truth. She feels like "a shadow or something like that, a stain or trace."

I've seen the shadow of a coachman rubbing the shadow of a coach with the shadow of a brush. (Dostoyevsky, "The Karamazov Brothers")

What tunnel are we going through? I said it was a tunnel that people built in the Japanese colonial time. One day you asked me what period I would like to visit if I could ride a time machine. There was nowhere I wanted to go but I did not want to disappoint you when you were so full of expectation so I said that I wanted to go back to the time when Dostoyevsky was writing "The Karamazov Brothers." But I said I didn't know what century that was. I might add that I seemed to be a shadow someone keeps dragging around, or something like that, a stain or trace. What would it feel like to become someone in the Japanese colonial time? I asked, if you could use a time machine one day, what period would you like to visit? You replied, a period when there are people building a tunnel of despair using hammers and chisels. I said we should visit the shadows of Marae building the shadows of a tunnel with the shadows of words.

"Marae Tunnel" full text

When a character in "The Karamazov Brothers" says "I've seen the shadow of a coachman rubbing the shadow of a coach with the shadow of a brush", he meant he had seen hell. In her poem "Marae Tunnel", An Hyeon-mi links this sentence to Marae Tunnel in the city of Yeosu. And this linkage weaves a net where the places and times, Russia in 1880 and Josu under Japanese rule in the 1920s, both signify hell. By simply rewriting the horrendous site of the people's pain where "people are building a tunnel of despair using hammers and chisels", the poet overcomes the stale and musty word 'hell'. This not only creates a new word that is specific and sensuous, but also increases sensitivity to the pain and humiliation of others and enables true solidarity. And the net, which grows longer day after day with repeated re-descriptions, is the words and traces of self-weaving by the girl who endured "the time taken to go roaming the pharmacy alley collecting sleeping pills"("Metamorphosis") and the guy, "no orphan but like an orphan" who is now cutting up "forty-nine winters"("Hi, Bear").

WHAT
THEY SAY
ABOUT
AN HYEON-MI

POET

Insofar as it gathers together and reflects on all the experiences and sensations of life as a problem of 'poetry(writing),' An's poetry is 'poetry about poetry,' but insofar as it closely records the birth and background of 'a dull poet/poem, a crazy poet/poem, a Zarathustra poet,' it is also poetry about the poetry of our time and the fate of the poet. The ultimate goal of An Hyeon-mi's poetry is to constantly adjust, reconstruct and repair this fate. It is one with her life. Hence, An Hyeon-mi's poetry as 'poetry about poetry' is inseparable from 'life-writing poetry.' The life sense tightly compressed into the poetry of An Hyeon-mi, the sense of a soft life compressing the details of reality are difficult to find in the poetry of other poets of the same generation.

Kim Su-ui, 'Night within Night' and 'A Hundred Years' Blackout':
a Study of An Hyeon-mi. MunhakDongne, 2014

K-Poet
Deep Work

Written by An Hyeon-Mi | **Translated by** Brother Anthony of Taizè
Published by ASIA Publishers | 445, Hoedong-gil, Paju-si, Gyeonggi-do, Korea
(Seoul Office: 161-1, Seodal-ro, Dongjak-gu, Seoul, Korea)
Homepage Address www.bookasia.org | **Tel** (822).821.5055 | **Fax** (822).821.5057
ISBN 979-11-5662-317-5 (set) | 979-11-5662-450-9 (04810)
First published in Korea by ASIA Publishers 2020

This book is published with the support of the Literature Translation Institute of Korea
(LTI Korea).

K-픽션 한국 젊은 소설

최근에 발표된 단편소설 중 가장 우수하고 흥미로운 작품을 엄선하여 출간하는 〈K-픽션〉은 한국문학의 생생한 현장을 국내외 독자들과 실시간으로 공유하고자 기획되었습니다. 원작의 재미와 품격을 최대한 살린 〈K-픽션〉 시리즈는 매 계절마다 새로운 작품을 선보입니다.

Through literature, you
bilingual Edition Modern

ASIA Publishers' carefully selected

Set 1	Set 2
 Division Industrialization Women	Liberty Love and Love Affairs South and North

Set 3	Set 4
Seoul Tradition Avant-Garde	Diaspora Family Humor

Search "bilingual edition

can meet the real Korea!
Korean Literature

22 keywords to understand Korean literature

Set 5

Relationships

Discovering

Everyday Life

Taboo and Desire

Set 6

Fate

Aesthetic Priests

The Naked in the

Colony

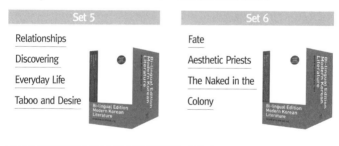

Set 7

Colonial Intellectuals Turned "Idiots"

Traditional Korea's Lost Faces

Before and After Liberation

Korea After the Korean War

korean literature"on Amazon!